Run!

First published in 2002 by
Franklin Watts
96 Leonard Street
London
EC2A 4XD

Franklin Watts Australia
56 O'Riordan Street
Alexandria
NSW 2015

A CIP catalogue record for this book is available
from the British Library.

ISBN 0 7496 4698 5 (hbk)
ISBN 0 7496 4705 1 (pbk)

Series Editor: Jackie Hamley
Series Advisor: Dr Barrie Wade
Cover Design: Jason Anscomb
Design: Peter Scoulding

Printed in Hong Kong

For my mother – SF

Run!

by Sue Ferraby and Fabiano Fiorin

W
FRANKLIN WATTS
LONDON•SYDNEY

Once a mouse called Jimjon
left his home in the rustling
leaves of the Tangly Wood.
He went night-visiting.

He crept under the tight fence
and through a grass stalk tunnel
to a little house.

Jimjon climbed the
cold stone steps.

He squeezed under the door.
He tiptoed over the prickly mat
into the kitchen.

All night long he ate crumbs in
the shadows under the stairs.

By and by the stars went pale.
The moon set. "I must get home
before the sun comes up,"
thought Jimjon.

Out of the shadows under
the stairs, Jimjon ran.

But a cat sat on the prickly mat.

So Jimjon couldn't get home.

Jimjon stopped. He listened.
He looked.

Jimjon saw that the cat was really
a coat, dropped in a heap.

Out of the shadows under
the stairs, across the prickly
mat, Jimjon ran.

But a giant stood on the cold stone
steps, guarding the door. Jimjon
couldn't get home.

Jimjon stopped. He listened.
He looked.

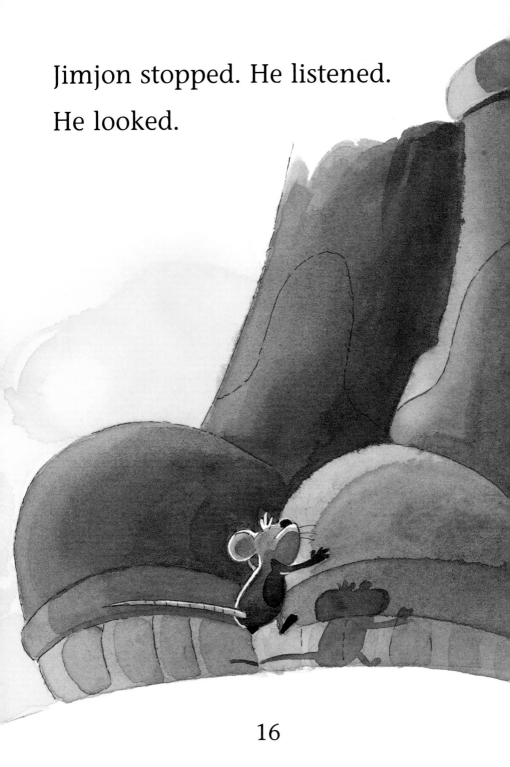

He saw that the giant feet were
not feet at all, but a pair of big
boots left outside.

Out of the shadows under the
stairs, across the prickly mat, down
the cold stone steps, Jimjon ran.

But a ghost spread its hands over the grass stalk tunnel, so Jimjon couldn't get home.

Jimjon stopped. He listened.
He looked.

He saw that the ghost was a piece
of paper, flapping in the wind.

Out of the shadows under the
stairs, across the prickly mat, down
the cold stone steps, through the
grass stalk tunnel, Jimjon ran.

But an owl sat near the tight
fence, watching even the smallest
thing that moved.

Jimjon stopped. He listened.
He looked.

The owl looked straight back at
him. Jimjon's heart froze with fear.

Then Jimjon saw that the owl was
the great sun rising through the
branches of the Tangly Wood.
It was morning.

Out of the shadows under the stairs, across the prickly mat, down the cold stone steps, through the grass stalk tunnel and under the tight fence, Jimjon ran.

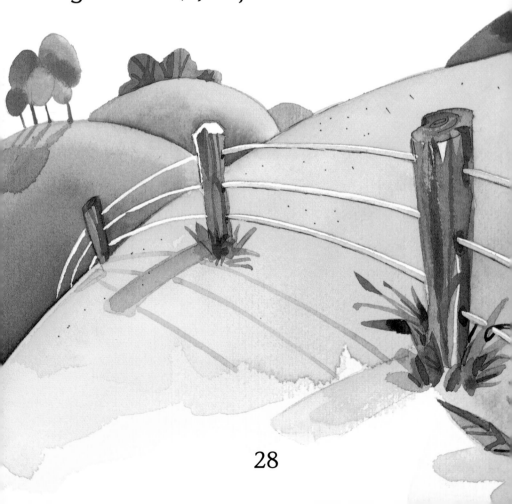

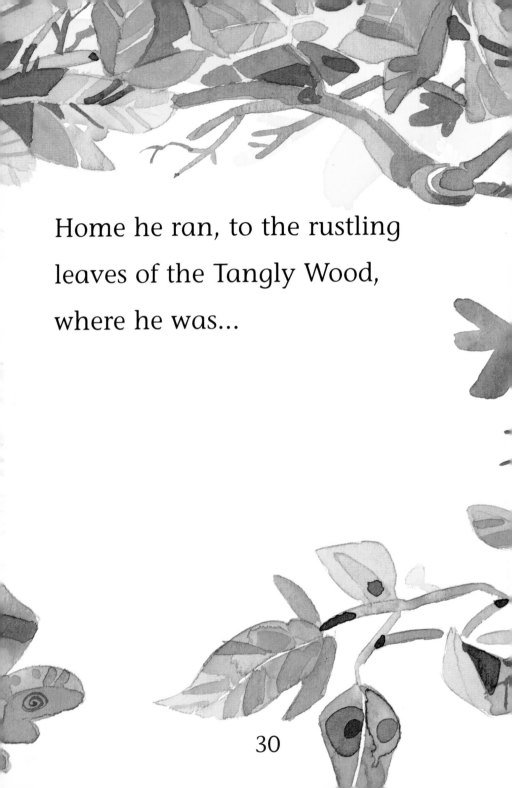

Home he ran, to the rustling
leaves of the Tangly Wood,
where he was...

...safe at last.

Hopscotch has been specially designed to fit the requirements of the National Literacy Strategy. It offers real books by top authors and illustrators for children developing their reading skills.

There are 12 Hopscotch stories to choose from:

Marvin, the Blue Pig
Written by Karen Wallace, illustrated by Lisa Williams
0 7496 4473 7 (hbk)
0 7496 4619 5 (pbk)

Plip and Plop
Written by Penny Dolan, illustrated by Lisa Smith
0 7496 4474 5 (hbk)
0 7496 4620 9 (pbk)

The Queen's Dragon
Written by Anne Cassidy, illustrated by Gwyneth Williamson
0 7496 4472 9 (hbk)
0 7496 4618 7 (pbk)

Flora McQuack
Written by Penny Dolan, illustrated by Kay Widdowson
0 7496 4475 3 (hbk)
0 7496 4621 7 (pbk)

Willie the Whale
Written by Joy Oades, illustrated by Barbara Vagnozzi
0 7496 4477 X (hbk)
0 7496 4623 3 (pbk)

Naughty Nancy
Written by Anne Cassidy, illustrated by Desideria Guicciardini
0 7496 4476 1 (hbk)
0 7496 4622 5 (pbk)

Run!
Written by Sue Ferraby, illustrated by Fabiano Fiorin
0 7496 4698 5 (hbk)
0 7496 4705 1 (pbk)

The Playground Snake
Written by Brian Moses, illustrated by David Mostyn
0 7496 4699 3 (hbk)
0 7496 4706 X (pbk)

"Sausages!"
Written by Anne Adeney, illustrated by Roger Fereday
0 7496 4700 0 (hbk)
0 7496 4707 8 (pbk)

The Truth about Hansel and Gretel
Written by Karina Law, illustrated by Elke Counsell
0 7496 4701 9 (hbk)
0 7496 4708 6 (pbk)

Pippin's Big Jump
Written by Hilary Robinson, illustrated by Sarah Warburton
0 7496 4703 5 (hbk)
0 7496 4710 8 (pbk)

Whose Birthday Is It?
Written by Sherryl Clark, illustrated by Jan Smith
0 7496 4702 7 (hbk)
0 7496 4709 4 (pbk)